THE
New Dog

BY Barbara Shook Hazen

PICTURES BY R. W. Alley

DIAL BOOKS FOR YOUNG READERS
NEW YORK

JJ
Hazen

For Elizabeth and William,
Catherine and Mary Martin,
and joyful Jack.
Explore the new and enjoy each other.
B. S. H.

For Amy and Christopher,
Pam and Eric—
dog lovers someday.
R. W. A.

Published by Dial Books for Young Readers
A Division of Penguin Books USA Inc.
375 Hudson Street
New York, New York 10014

Text copyright © 1997 by Barbara Shook Hazen
Pictures copyright © 1997 by R. W. Alley
Designed by Ann Finnell
Printed in Hong Kong
First Edition
1 3 5 7 9 10 8 6 4 2

Library of Congress Cataloging in Publication Data
Hazen, Barbara Shook.
The new dog / by Barbara Shook Hazen ; pictures by R. W. Alley
p.   cm.
Summary: When Tootsie, a small, pampered dog,
joins Danny Dougle's Dogwalking Group, he is
teased and tormented by the other dogs until
he wins their respect by foiling a robbery.
ISBN 0-8037-1812-8. — ISBN 0-8037-1813-6 (lib. bdg.)
[1. Dogs—Fiction. 2. Behavior—Fiction.]
I. Alley, Robert W., ill. II. Title.
PZ7.H314975Ne 1997 [E]—dc20 94-34964 CIP AC

The artwork was rendered in pen-and-ink and watercolor.

Miss Pettibone fluffed Tootsie's fur, buffed his nails, and put bows on both ears.

"Today is a special day," she said. "Today is your first day with Danny's Dogwalking Group. You're a big dog now. You're big enough to make friends and learn new things." The excited way she said it made Tootsie wriggle with pleasure.

"Be a good dog," Miss Pettibone told Tootsie at the door. "Take care of my precious Tootsie," she told Danny Dougle.

The old dogs eyeballed each other. "We'll take care of him all right," the biggest snorted. The others nodded.

The door closed and Danny introduced Tootsie.
"Tootsie, I'd like you to meet Bruiser, the biggest; Rex,
the oldest; Fleet, the fastest; Cleo, a blue-ribbon winner;
Bagels, our chowhound; Trixie, who was with the circus;
and Pepé and Pal, the terrier twins."

The old dogs sniffed Tootsie suspiciously.

Tootsie barked and bowed politely, which always pleased
Miss Pettibone. His bark came out a scared squeak.

The old dogs howled.

"That's enough," Danny said—to Tootsie.

"Walk," Danny said, without a pat or, "Pretty please."

The old dogs stepped out smartly. Tootsie lagged behind and looked in every store window, the way he always did with Miss Pettibone.

"Walk!" Danny repeated, tugging at Tootsie's leash. "Try to keep up."

At the corner there was a mud puddle. The old dogs sloshed through it. Tootsie planted his paws and waited to be carried across, the way he always was by Miss Pettibone.

"Walk, Tootsie," said Danny. "Pick up your own paws."

Tootsie did and got a pebble in his left paw.

"See," Tootsie whimpered and showed Danny.

"And no whining!" Danny added as he picked out the pebble. Tootsie sulked. Miss Pettibone would have kissed his paw and carried him.

"Puppy paws!" the old dogs all snorted.

"Precious Tootsie, want to play footsie?" Bruiser smiled and held out his big rough paw. To be friendly, Tootsie held out his small paw.

Bruiser smacked it hard, toppling Tootsie into the gutter.

Danny didn't see what Bruiser did. But he saw Tootsie's tomato-stained coat and the strand of spaghetti dangling from one ear.

"No, Tootsie," Danny scolded. "On the sidewalk, not in the gutter. Together is the way we walk."

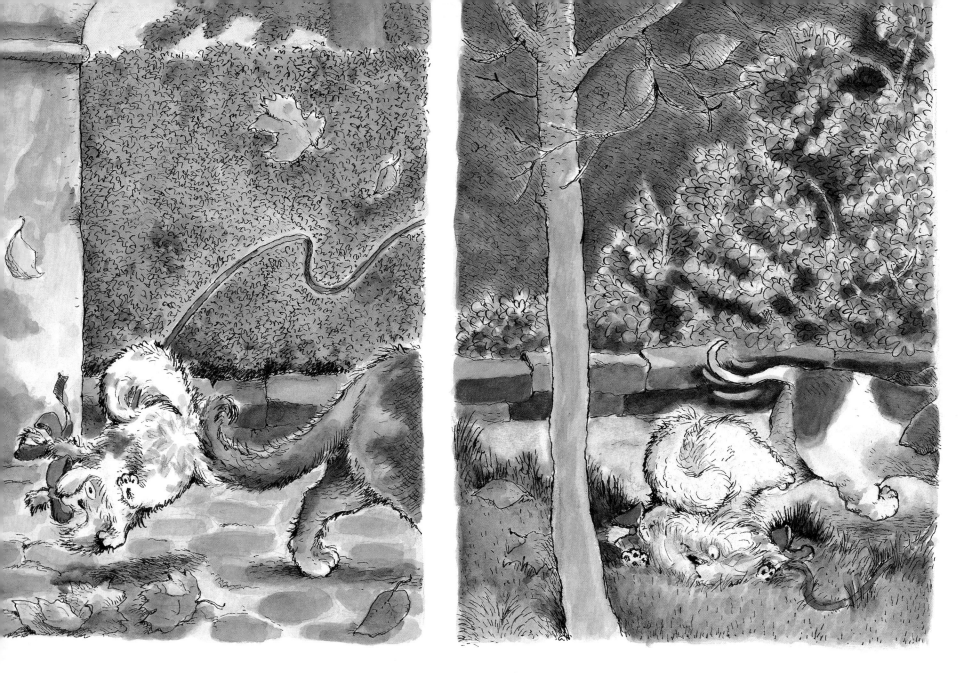

In the park the old dogs teased Tootsie when Danny wasn't looking.
Rex tail-thumped him, and Bagels side-bumped him.

Fleet ran rings around him and tangled his leash.
"How did that happen?" Danny asked, frowning.

Cleo totally ignored Tootsie, except for yawning in his face.

Pepé and Pal nipped off Tootsie's ear bows, which Trixie juggled behind Danny's back.

Danny didn't see that, but he saw Tootsie trying to retrieve them. "Down, Tootsie," he said. "Be a good dog or I'll have to take you home."

As they walked, the old dogs snorted, "Puppy paws, precious shrimp! Tootsie, wootsie, what a wimp!"

As they left the park, Bruiser, the biggest tease, whispered, "Look in the fountain to see something funny."

Tootsie leaned over to look. Bruiser shoved Tootsie into the water and howled.

Tootsie emerged yipping and showing his teeth.

"For shame, Tootsie," Danny scolded. "You are a naughty dog. I am going to have to take you home immediately and tell Miss Pettibone."

Tootsie refused to budge.

"Walk!" Danny commanded.
"I mean it, Tootsie."

Tootsie did not move.

"WALK!" Danny said louder,
and pulled harder.

Tootsie pulled too, the opposite
way.

Suddenly there was a loud POP!
Then a voice shouted, "STOP!"

"STAY!" Danny yelled at the top
of his lungs.

Then he yelled, "DOWN!" and
yanked at all the leashes, pulling
the dogs behind a parked truck.

Tootsie, tired of being scolded
and told what to do, resisted.
His collar snapped
and he bolted free
into the street.

"TOOTSIE, COME!
COME, TOOTSIE!"
Danny's voice was
now a scream.

Tootsie ran on, right in front of a man running with a shopping bag.

"Outta my way, fluffermutt," the mean-looking man snarled and tried to kick Tootsie out of his way.

Tootsie snarled back and sank his teeth into the man's leg.

"Mad dog!" the man yelled as he fell.

Tootsie held on tightly as sirens screeched, passersby shrieked,
and a policeman raced to the scene.

"Don't make a move!" the policeman ordered. Tootsie closed his eyes, waiting for the worst.

"Anything you say can be held against you . . . " Tootsie heard the words and the click of cold steel, but he felt warm fingers.

Tootsie opened his eyes and saw the man, handcuffed and kicking. He saw Miss Pettibone gasping and starting across the street. Most amazing of all, Tootsie saw the old dogs still cowering behind the parked truck. He also saw a puddle of piddle under a shamefaced, droopy-tailed Bruiser.

The policeman gently stroked Tootsie and said, "Good, brave dog! You nabbed Light-fingered Louie *and* the loot! But who do you belong to? I don't see a collar."

"Me!" Miss Pettibone ran up and hugged Tootsie.

"My Dogwalking Group," Danny piped up proudly.

"Us!" the old dogs barked, and gave Tootsie the tails-up sign—all except Bruiser, who was still cowering and trying to cover his puddle.

That night Tootsie got extra
pats, Doggie Delights, and his
pillow plumped by
Miss Pettibone.

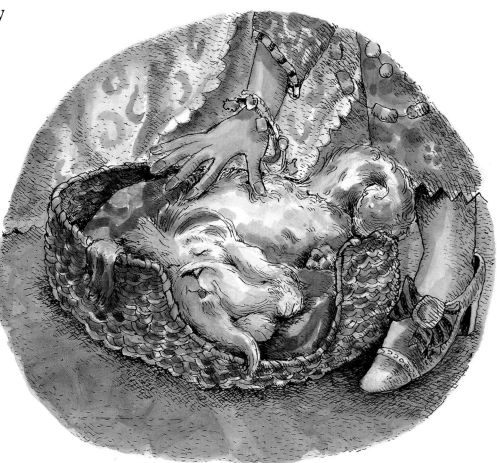

The next day Tootsie was eager to go
with Danny and the old dogs, now new friends.
After Tootsie was picked up, a *new* new dog joined
the group. He drooled and shook and tried to hide.

"Take care of Tiny Timmy," the new dog's person said. "It's his first day and he's shy."

The old dogs sniffed suspiciously. "We'll take care of him all right." Bruiser eyeballed the others and snorted.

"Not if I take care of him first," Tootsie said. He stepped in front of Bruiser and walked up to the new dog.

"Welcome," he said. "Don't worry. Their bluff is bigger than their bite, especially the big one's. You'll do just fine!"